U0028809

Cyber

※本書提供高效能閱覽模式：
請將書本貼到臉上使用最新ＶＲ科技

⇨ 序

安安 你好哇

目錄

BONUS：找不同
你好啊，真沒想到你可以看到這裡呢，
不過就到此為止了，
接下來是考驗眼球的時間！
P.151

成為人見人愛的社交之王

好人緣使你事半功倍

「我是世上最謙虛的人！」
"I'm the most humble man on earth!"

humble

謙虛的，謙遜的

「嘿！你男友完全是我的菜耶！
他單身嗎？」
"Heyyy! Your boyfriend is totally my typ
Is he single?"

boyfriend

男朋友

「我們處女座的人沒有一個信星座的！」
We virgos don't believe in horoscopes!"

virgo
處女座

「嘿！不要一直展開我的水餃！」
"Hey! Stop unfolding my dumplings!"

unfold

打開；展開；攤開

「嘿！快點停止攪拌我的布丁！」
"Hey! Stop stirring my pudding!"

stir

（用湯匙等）攪動，攪拌

9

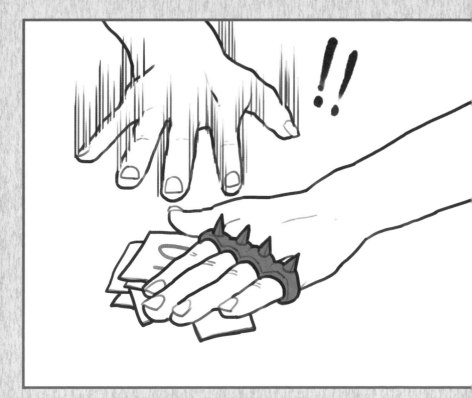

配戴手指虎玩心臟病
讓輸家更深刻嚐到失敗的滋味。
Wear brass knuckles when playing slapjack to ensure the losers get a clear taste of their defeat.

brass knuckle

手指虎

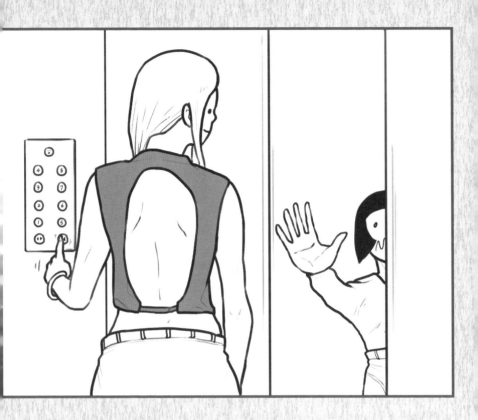

連續按關門鍵以享受更多私人空間。

Press the 'close door' button repeatedly to enjoy more personal space.

repeatedly

反覆地，重複地

「快殺了愛莉絲！
她是個殭屍，只是還沒被咬！」
*"Hurry up and kill Alice! She's a zombie!
She just hasn't been bitten by one yet."*

zombie

殭屍

Cher超討厭Josh！
就算Josh沒講話時Cher也會叫他閉嘴。

Cher hates Josh so much that she tells him to shut up even when he is not talking.

hate

嫌惡，不喜歡

「Jimmy，你掉到岩漿裡了！」
"Jimmy, you fell into the lava!"

lava
（火山噴出的）岩漿，熔岩；火山岩

14

「嗎好你？Joe，嘿！」
"Going it how's? Joe, hey!"

hey
嘿

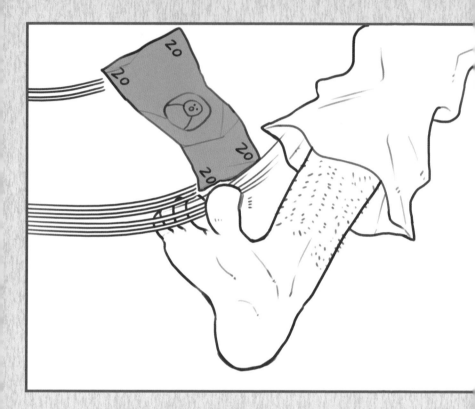

**Mark沒能幫Cindy接住被
突然刮起的狂風吹走的20鎂。**
**Mark failed to catch Cindy's 20 dollars
for her when the wind suddenly blew.**

wind

風

Kent叔叔的棺材下葬時
我們放了俄羅斯方塊的音樂。
We played the Tetris theme song as we
lowered Uncle Kent's coffin into his grave.

tetris
俄羅斯方塊

與外國人成為好麻吉

當ABC原來這麼容易

「關門！！！！！！！！！」
"CLOSE THE DOOR!!!!!!!!"

door

門

「我要跟你說幾次？不要用洗衣機洗碗！

*"How many times do I have to tell you
not to use the washing machine
to wash the dishes?"*

washing machine

洗衣機

「Anna，你又用廚房手套保暖。」
「這是襪子，白癡！」

"Anna, you are wearing oven mitts
to keep your hands warm again."
"These are socks, idiot!"

oven mitt

（廚房用）隔熱手套

「我們去跟蹤那棵樹！」
"Let's follow that tree!"

follow
尾隨；跟蹤

「我鄰居是個跟蹤狂！
他每天都住在隔壁。」
"My neighbor is a stalker! He always
lives next door."

stalker

跟蹤者；（尤指）跟蹤騷擾他人者

「我是客人耶！
你怎麼可以叫我付錢？！」
"I'm a customer!
How dare you ask me to pay my bill?!"

bill

帳單

24

美國風情

看過這篇都不用去美國了

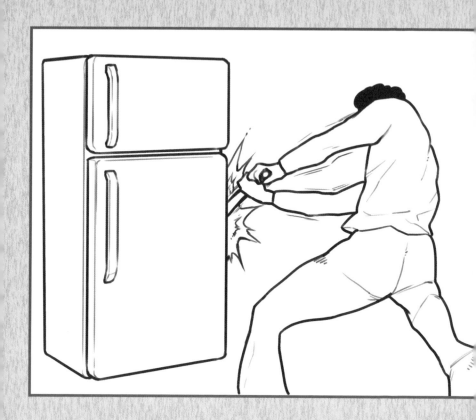

全壘打啦！！！！！！！！
HOME RUN!!!!!!!!

home run

全壘打

「Dave！快停止吃那些香菸！
它們不是薯條。」
"Dave! Stop eating all the cigarettes,
those are not fries."

cigarette

香菸，紙煙

在口罩上打一個洞
就可以隨時喝飲料了。
**Punch a hole in the mask to
drink at any time!**

punch a hole

穿孔,穿洞

28

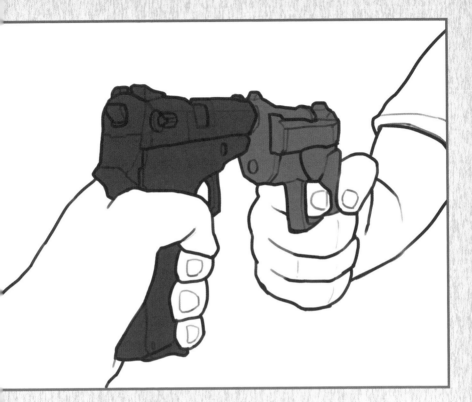

在對方射擊時用槍口抵住槍口以掠奪他的子彈！

Right when your opponent is about to fire his pistol, hold your pistol against his to steal his bullet!

bullet

子彈

自我提升篇

強迫自己進化！跳脫肉體的極限！

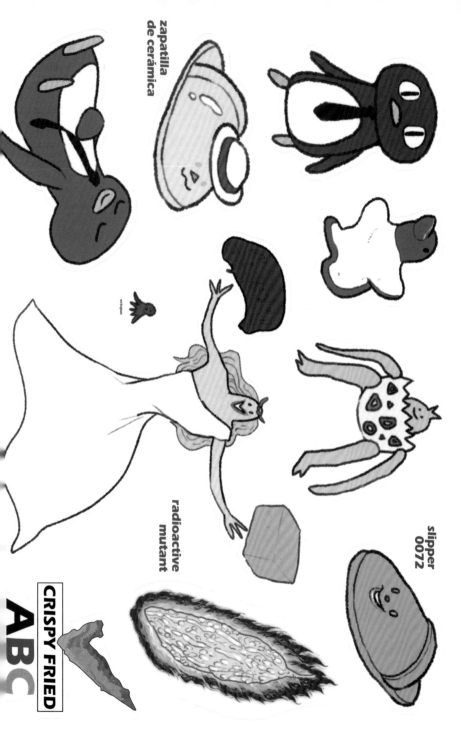

zapatilla
de cerámica

octopus

radioactive
mutant

slipper
0072

CRISPY FRIED
ABC

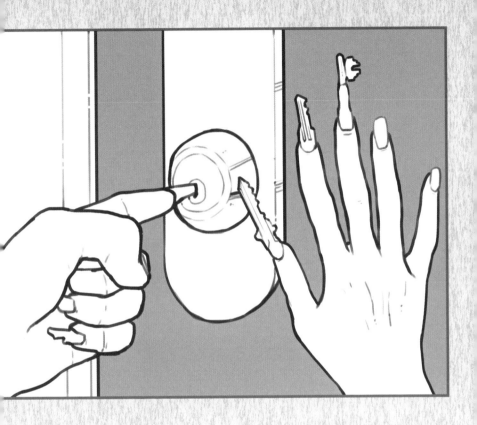

把指甲刻成鑰匙就不會忘記帶出門。
Carve your nails into keys so you will never forget to bring them.

carve
刻‧雕刻

同時戴隱形眼鏡與眼鏡來看得更清楚！
Wear contacts under your glasses
to see more clearly!

clearly
清楚地

已經盯著鏡子4小時了
還是看不到自己眨眼的那瞬間。

ve been staring at the mirror for 4 hours
and I still can't catch the moment
when I blink.

blink

眨眼睛

茶葉蛋的滷汁可不要浪費了，通通喝完

Do not waste the marinade for tea egg.
Finish it all!

marinade

滷汁

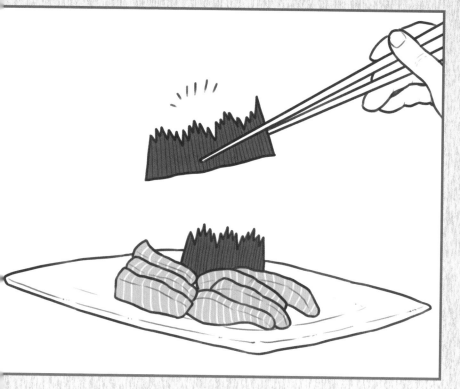

為了飲食要均衡，
生魚片時可別忘了也吃隨之附贈的葉子。
**For a balanced diet,
don't forget to eat the leaves
that come with your sashimi.**

sashimi

生魚片

把全身的力量集中在小指
以打出強烈的一拳！
**Focus all of your power on your pinky
to throw a powerful punch!**

pinky

小指；小妞妞

溺水時，游到岸邊可降低死亡風險。

When you are drowning, reduce the risk of dying by swimming to the shore.

drowning

溺水

Sydney是個非常勇敢的女人！
她會玩名為「關掉鬧鐘後閉上眼睛」
的危險運動。

Sydney is a very brave woman!
She plays a dangerous sport called
"closing your eyes after turning off your alarm"

brave

勇敢的，英勇的

「來看看這個我在淘寶買的
聽診器有多耐用！」
"Let's see how durable
this stethoscope I bought from
Taobao is!"

durable

持久的，耐久的

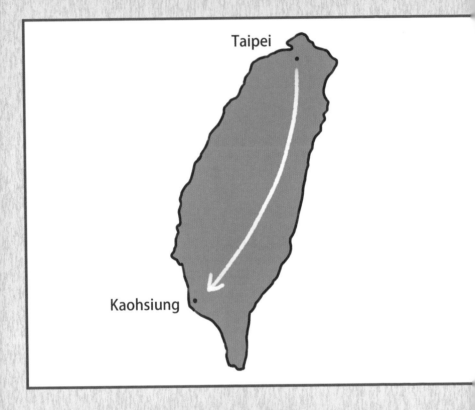

如果走得快，
15分鐘便能從台北走到高雄。
If you walk fast enough, you can walk
from Taipei to Kaohsiung in 15 minutes

walk

走；步行

善心小舉動

一起來把世界變得更美好

「請你戴口罩！你咀嚼的聲音太大了！」
"Please wear a mask!
You are chewing too loud! "

chew

嚼，咀嚼，嚼碎

「外帶的水餃你給我加醬油幹麼？！」
"Why are you adding soy sauce
to my takeout dumplings?!"

takeout

外帶

「如果在便當裡發現三色冷凍蔬菜的話，
請立刻通報當地警察。」
"Please inform the local police ASAP
if you find frozen mixed vegetables
in your lunch box."

frozen mixed vegetables

三色冷凍蔬菜

善良的Harold總是幫旅館把
床單跟床墊訂在一起以防止鬆脫。
**Kind-hearted Harold always staples
the hotel's bed sheet to the mattress
so it won't come off.**

staple
用訂書針釘

VOCABULARY：ROOM
房間中的常見單字

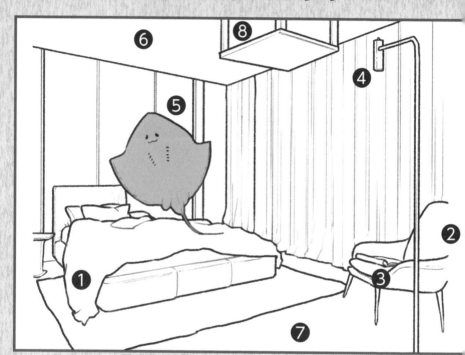

1. bed 床
2. chair 椅子
3. book 書
4. floor lamp 立燈
5. stingray 魟魚

6. loud and rude upstairs neighbor
   又吵又無禮的樓上鄰居
7. carpet 地毯
8. desk 書桌

VOCABULARY：BODY (centipede)
蜈蚣身體的常見單字

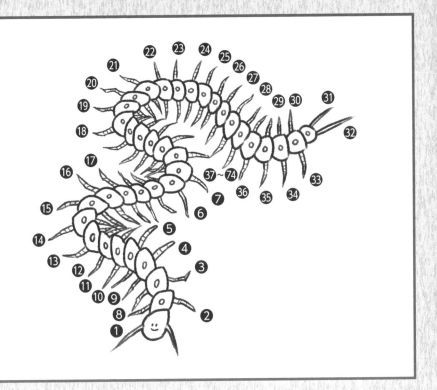

1. leg 腳	12. leg 腳	23. leg 腳	34. leg 腳	45. leg 腳	56. leg 腳	67. leg 腳
2. leg 腳	13. leg 腳	24. leg 腳	35. leg 腳	46. leg 腳	57. leg 腳	68. leg 腳
3. leg 腳	14. leg 腳	25. leg 腳	36. leg 腳	47. leg 腳	58. leg 腳	69. leg 腳
4. leg 腳	15. leg 腳	26. leg 腳	37. leg 腳	48. leg 腳	59. leg 腳	70. leg 腳
5. leg 腳	16. leg 腳	27. leg 腳	38. leg 腳	49. leg 腳	60. leg 腳	71. leg 腳
6. leg 腳	17. leg 腳	28. leg 腳	39. leg 腳	50. leg 腳	61. leg 腳	72. leg 腳
7. leg 腳	18. leg 腳	29. leg 腳	40. leg 腳	51. leg 腳	62. leg 腳	73. leg 腳
8. leg 腳	19. leg 腳	30. leg 腳	41. leg 腳	52. leg 腳	63. leg 腳	74. leg 腳
9. leg 腳	20. leg 腳	31. leg 腳	42. leg 腳	53. leg 腳	64. leg 腳	
10. leg 腳	21. leg 腳	32. leg 腳	43. leg 腳	54. leg 腳	65. leg 腳	
11. leg 腳	22. leg 腳	33. leg 腳	44. leg 腳	55. leg 腳	66. leg 腳	

DIY!
延虛線剪下以獲得可愛章魚，方便搞丟

VOCABULARY：BODY
身體的常見單字

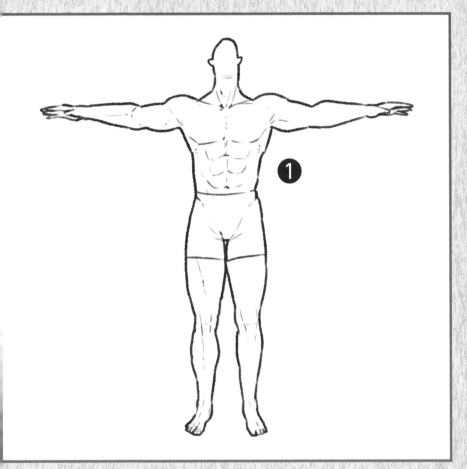

1. whole body　全身

職場加薪密技

昨天還是員工，今天升職成老闆

「陳先生，請不要沒穿襯衫就來面試。」
"Mr. Chen, please don't show up to an interview without a shirt."

interview

面試；面談

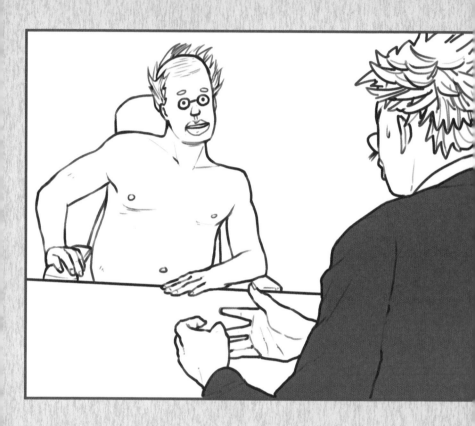

「陳先生…」
"Mr. Chen..."

Chen

陳

快速吸入大量空氣來使
討厭的同事陷入窒息狀態！
Quickly inhale a great amount of air
to suffocate the coworkers you hate!

inhale
吸氣；吸入

「辛苦了！今天在場的大家都做得很好
除了全部人。」
"Good job! All of you did well today,
except for everyone."

except

除了

「我有20%的機率百分之百是對的。」
"20% of the time I'm 100% correct."

percent
百分之…（符號為%）

「搶劫哇！！！他付了錢，
然後把他買的東西拿走了！」
"Robbery! He paid me,
then took the items he paid for!!!"

robbery

搶劫；盜竊

為了防止市民在路上突然溺死，
多數救生員轉行當陸地救生員。

To prevent citizens from suddenly rowning on the streets, many lifeguards chose to become ground lifeguards.

drown

溺死

**John啟動高速模式了！
他是全辦公室中最快的人。**
**John just activated High-Speed Mode!
He is the fastest man in the office.**

office

辦公室

「我們算出來的數據非常大！
快要到無限了。」
"The numeric data we derived was
very large! It's almost reaching infinity."

infinity

無限

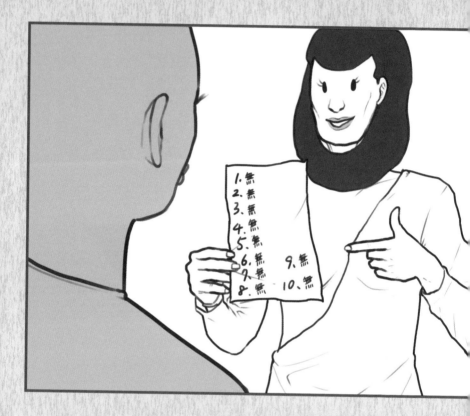

「嘿，Jasmine，你看！
我在這張紙上列出了10個你的優點！」
"Hey, Jasmine, look!
I listed your 10 strengths on this paper."

list

列舉；列出

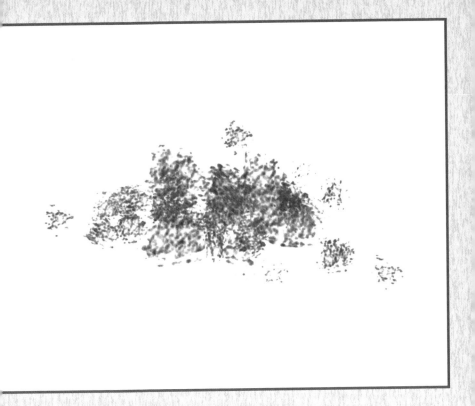

客戶就像樹枝，放火燒就會變成灰燼。
Clients are like tree branches; they will
turn into ash if you set them on fire.

ash
灰，灰燼

人生哲理

消化不良吃消化餅乾消化不了消化餅乾

「要是我沒有輸的話就贏了！」
"I'd win if I didn't lose!"

lose

輸掉（比賽）；敗北，失利

「把橘子吃掉之後橘子就不見了！？」
"The tangerine disappeared after I ate it?!"

tangerine

橘子

「電風扇葉片在我把它打開後
就不見了？！」
"When I turn the electric fan on,
its fan blades disappear?!"

electric fan

電風扇

「如果水髒了能不能用水洗滌乾淨呢？

"Can dirty water be cleansed by water?"

cleanse

清洗；淨化，洗滌

湯匙就只是小的碗罷了。
Spoons are just tiny bowls.

bowl
碗

67

生存之道

多活一天算一天

在刀上加裝雷射瞄準器來提高命中率！
Attach a laser sight on your sword to increase accuracy!

laser sight
雷射瞄準器

用手走路，這樣別人就無法靠
你的腳印追蹤你。
**Walk on your hands so no one can
track you with your footprints.**

footprint

腳印，足跡

迷路的時候，聽聽看北極的聲音
來判斷北邊是什麼方向。

When you are lost, listen to the sound
from the North Pole to find north.

North Pole

北極

為了確保孩童安全，
我們在公園新建了更多的路燈。
To make sure the kids are safe,
we added
more streetlamps around the park.

streetlamp

街燈，路燈

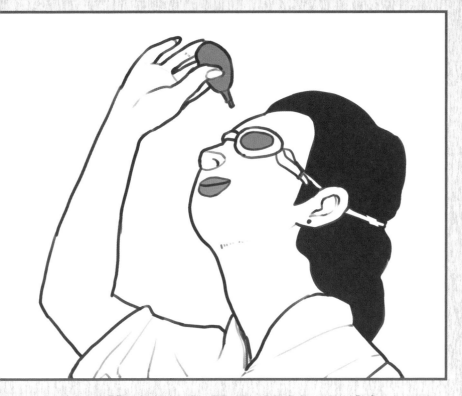

點眼藥水前先戴上蛙鏡以避免其帶來的刺痛感。

To avoid the burning sensation from eye drops, wear swimming goggles beforehand.

eye drops

眼藥水

「為什麼手機連不上網哇？
阿！我知道了！上google查查看。」
*"Why can't I connect to the internet?
Oh, I know! Let me google it."*

google

(v.) 搜索（利用Google搜索引擎在網路上查找資料）

唱越大聲麥克風就拿越遠，
別人才不會聽到你難聽的歌聲。
Hold your mic farther as you sing louder
so people won't hear your awful voice.

mic

麥克風（microphone 的非正式說法）

美妝達人

省下微整儲備金，小資也能做美人

想要香氣逼人？噴一些火鍋湯在身上！
Wanna smell fantastic? Go ahead and spray some hot pot soup on yourself!

hot pot
火鍋

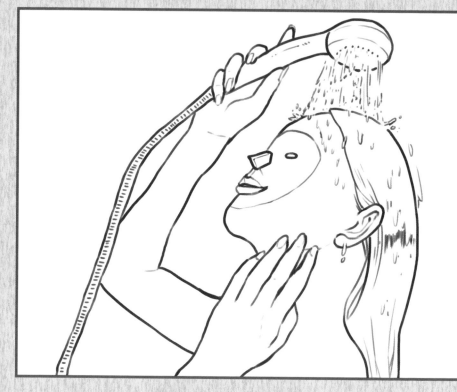

連續洗三次澡，
這樣接下來三天就不用洗澡了。
**Take 3 showers in a row so that
you don't have to take another shower
for the next 3 days.**

in a row

接連地；連續地

化完妝後立刻洗臉以避免毛孔堵塞。
Wash your face immediately after you put on makeup to avoid clogged pores.

pore
毛孔；氣孔；小孔

「我把指甲油塗在鼻子上，
效果比遮瑕膏更好！」
"I put nail polish on my nose and
it worked better than concealer!"

concealer

遮瑕膏

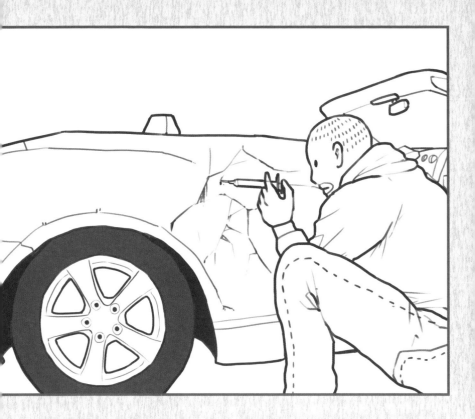

施打玻尿酸是無法填補車子的凹陷的。
Injecting dermal filler won't fix the dent in your car.

dent
（物體表面上的）坑，凹陷

節日

日子跟著節氣過，歲月才有層次感

「豪龍，快點！我們也要慶祝節日！
粽子交給我，你去做一條龍舟！」
"Hurry, Hao-Long!
We need to celebrate the festival today!
I'll get the rice dumpling ready,
you go craft the dragon boat!"

rice dumpling

粽子

單身的好處就是你可以幫要去
約會的同事們加班。
**The perk of being single is that
you can work overtime to finish projects
for coworkers going on their dates.**

single

單身

「這是我們今天幫Gary掃墓時拍的照片。」
「阿Gary怎麼沒去？」
"These are the pictures we took today
while sweeping Gary's tomb."
Oh, why didn't Gary go with you guys?"

sweep

掃；清掃，打掃

「這必須得幫我加薪了吧…」
"I should get a raise for this..."

raise
加薪

實用句子：面對醫生

If I die I will be very pissed!
如果我死了我可是會很生氣的！

It gets very uncomfortable if I don't blink
my eyes for 10 minutes.
我只要10分鐘不眨眼就會很不舒服。

I always almost die choking when I drink water
while laughing. Is there a medicine for that?
我一面笑一面喝水都會差點嗆死！有沒有藥可以醫？

I'm afraid of pain, can we not do X-ray?
我很怕痛，可以不要照X光嗎？

My hair hurts!
頭髮好痛！

VOCABULARY：MONEY
錢的常見單字

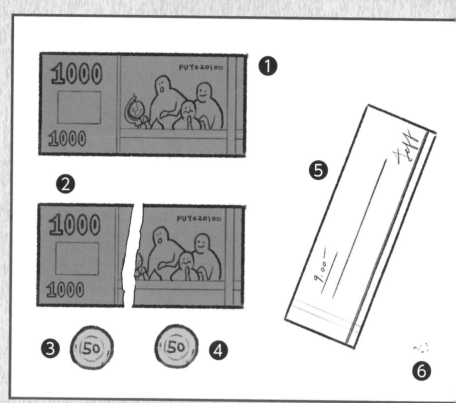

1. $1000 bill   一千元鈔票
2. $500 bill   五百元鈔票
3. $50 coin   五十元硬幣
4. 800 $50 coins (top view) 800個五十元硬幣（俯視圖）
5. 9 dollar check   9元支票
6. your savings   你的存款

DIY!
超值！延虛線剪下以獲得海浪

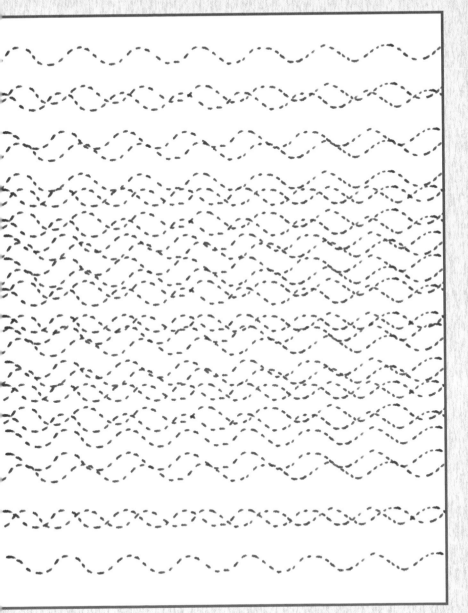

省錢小撇步

當巴菲特真簡單

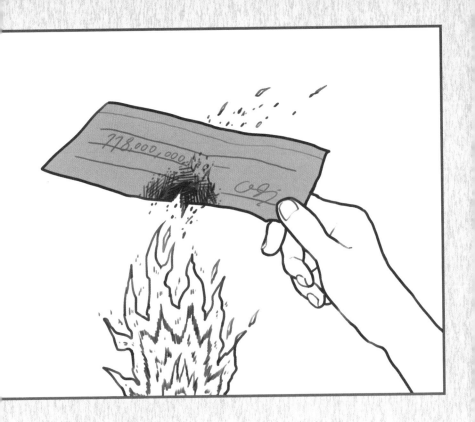

切勿用火燒支票！會不見。
Do not burn the check with fire!
It will disappear.

check
支票

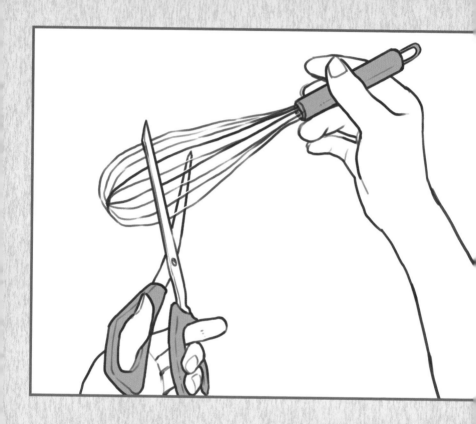

將打蛋器剪半，輕鬆做出頭部按摩器！
Easily make a head massager by cutting a whisk in half!

whisk
（蛋、奶油等的）攪拌器

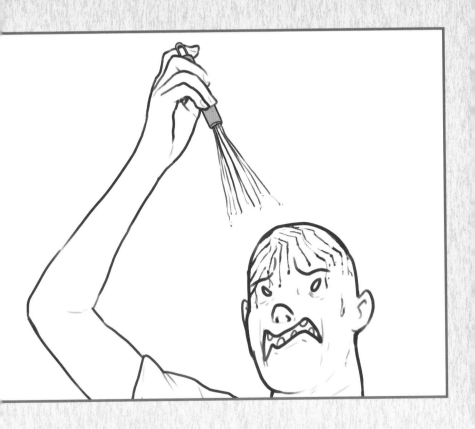

「誰買的頭部按摩器啊？！太尖了！」
Who the hell bought this head massager?!
It's way too sharp!"

sharp
鋒利的；尖的

「我剛剛把提款卡放進ATM可以領出錢，
你現在試試把錢放到ATM裡面能不能
領出一張提款卡。」

"I just took out money from the ATM
using my debit card. Now you try putting mone
in the ATM and see if you get a debit card."

debit card

提款卡

「誰要花錢加油阿。」
"Ain't nobody gonna pay for gas."

汽油

糾正並複習之前樂透券上沒中的數字，
為下次的大獎做準備。

**Review and fix the incorrect numbers
from the previous lottery tickets
to prepare yourself for the next jackpot.**

lottery

彩券，樂透

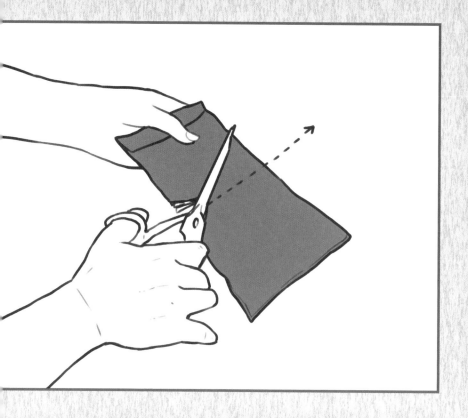

打開紅包最快的方式就是
直接用剪刀剪開。
The fastest way to open a
red envelope is to cut it with scissors.

scissors
剪刀

「不！你不能拿走我的書！
這是我找到的！我在你抽屜裡找到的！
"No, you can't have my book!
I found it! I found it in your drawer!"

drawer

抽屜

校園實境

多益都考一百分

「上課時間不要講話！！！！」
"No talking in class!!!!"

talk

講話

考試時攜帶筆刀並把寫好的問題
挖掉，避免別人抄你的答案。
**Cut off your answers with an
X-Acto knife to prevent others
from cheating during an exam.**

X-Acto knife

筆刀

「老師！我對自己好失望！我竟然只考98分！
「喔好，那我把你當掉。」
"Teacher! I'm so disappointed in myself!
I only scored 98 on the test!"
"Okay, I will fail you then."

fail

評定（學生）不及格

自從把接力棒換成炸藥之後，
我們的隊伍就成了大隊接力賽的常勝軍。

Ever since we replaced the baton
with dynamite, our team has been a
frequent tag team race winner.

baton

接力棒

科技始終來自於

惰性

我們發明了攜帶型筆芯！
每一根都只有1公分！超輕！超好帶！
We have invented portable lead!
Every piece is just 1 cm long!
Very light! Very easy to carry!

portable
便於攜帶的，手提式的；輕便的

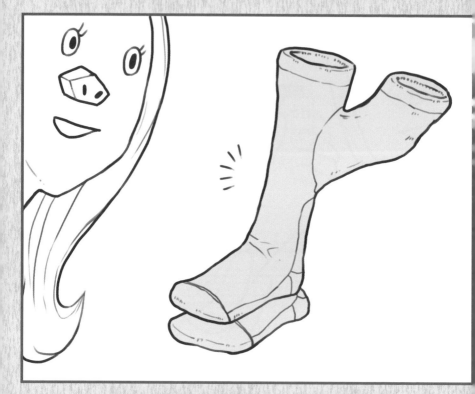

這款新型的襪子可以解決
洗完衣服後總會少一支的問題！

**These newly designed socks
will prevent one sock from going missing
after doing the laundry!**

socks
襪子

這款新型的涼鞋可以解決
其中一支總是被海浪沖走的問題！

These newly designed sandals
solve the problem of one getting
washed away by the waves!

sandal

涼鞋；拖鞋

我們會定期更新應用程式，帶給你
更愚蠢的使用體驗。立即下載最新版本，
享用過去所有的程式錯誤，以及更多新的。
**We update this app regularly
to make it stupider for you.
Get the latest version with all the old bugs
included and many new ones.**

bug
（程式中的）錯誤

「我們最新研發的相機
可是有手機的功能。」
"Our latest invention boasts a camera
that comes with
standard phone features."

latest

最新的

二手螢幕！
除了黑屏以外其餘功能一切正常。
Second-hand monitor!
Other than the black screen,
all other functions work just fine.

second-hand

二手的

可憐

可憐勹人

「電影院的聲音效果太大了！
根本沒辦法好好睡覺。」
"The sound effects in the movie
theatre are too loud!
I can't even get a good sleep."

sound effect

聲音效果，音效

112

時光俠可以穿越時光去未來，
但也會隨穿越的時間變老。
**Time Man can travel forward in time
but will age accordingly as well.**

age
變老

「我每天一起床就失眠！
從早上7點失眠到晚上11點才能睡。」
"When I wake up every day,
I get insomnia! I have trouble
falling asleep from 7am to 11 pm."

insomnia

失眠

「她已經連續回你三次「哈哈」了！
已經沒救了！不要再繼續密她了！」

"She texted back "haha" to you
3 times in a row already!
It's hopeless! Stop messaging her!"

hopeless

無望的，沒救，沒有辦法的

115

「我的指紋跟記憶中的不一樣！」
"My fingerprint is different from what I remembered!"

fingerprint

指紋

「哈哈哈！他不會發ㄌ的音！
真是個乳蛇！」

*"Hahaha! He can't even pronounce
the L sound! What a ruser!"*

pronounce

發（音），讀（音）

「在10點前起床應該屬於
違法的行為才對吧。」
*"It should be illegal
to wake up before 10 AM."*

illegal

非法的，違法的

Betty有懼高症！
她不敢穿鞋子。
Betty has acrophobia!
She is afraid to wear shoes.

acrophobia
懼高症

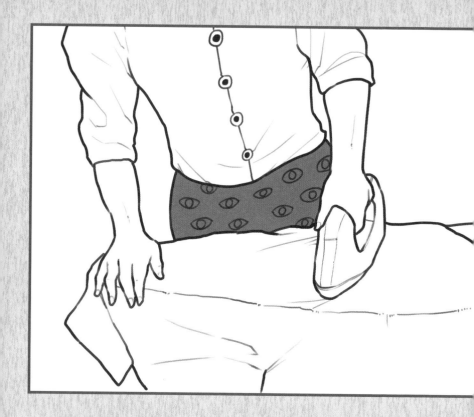

「把老公謀殺之後竟然要自己燙衣服。
"Can't believe I have to iron my shirts myself after murdering my husband."

husband

丈夫

「我買了一個新的迴力鏢
但是沒辦法把舊的丟走。」
"I got a new boomerang but
I can't throw the old one away."

boomerang

迴力鏢

「王八蛋把我盜來的帳號偷回去了，死小偷！缺德。」

"This asshole stole his account back after I hacked it from him! Damn robber! What a dick!"

hack

駭入，破解

糧食與食材運用

末日生存指南（大饑荒時請看）

腸胃炎期間建議吃溫和的食物，
例如小兔子。

**When you have a stomach flu,
it is recommended to eat
mild food such as bunnies.**

bunny

小兔子

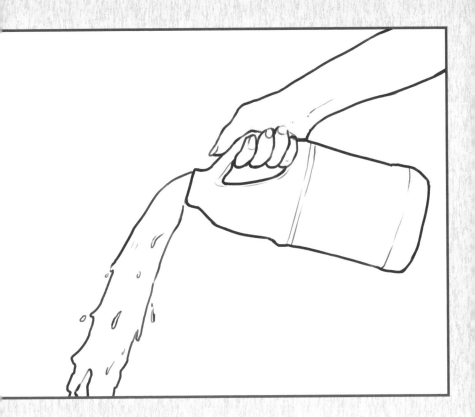

牛奶很容易過期！先倒掉一半再買。
Milk expires quickly!
Pour away half before buying it.

expire
過期

「水好濕！」
"Water is so wet!"

wet

濕的

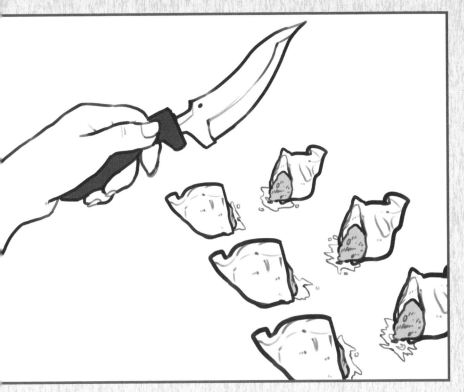

勿受騙！食用前先將所有餃子割開，以確保裡面確實有餡料。

Avoid getting scammed!
Cut open each dumpling before eating to ensure all of them have fillings.

filling
餡料

奶奶都用火車來搗胡蘿蔔泥。
**Grandma purées carrots
by using the train.**

purée
把（水果或蔬菜）壓（或碾）成泥

在我們國家，強迫囚犯
吃苦瓜是一種極刑。
In our country, forcing the prisoners
to eat bitter melons is an extreme
penalty.

extreme penalty

極刑，酷刑

當鍋子起火時表示該關爐火了。
When the pot is on fire, it indicates that it's time to turn off the stove.

stove

（用於烹飪的）爐灶；火爐

洋芋片太脆了！敲碎！

Potato chips are too crispy! Smash'em!

crispy

酥脆的

實用句子：餐廳

Can I order from the menu I brought from another restaurant?
我可不可以從其他餐廳帶來的菜單上點菜呢？

Why can't I come inside the kitchen?
為什麼我不能進來廚房呢？

If I don't order, how long will I have to wait to get my food?
如果我不點菜的話，要等多久才會上菜呢？

Noodle soups usually don't taste very dry.
湯麵通常吃起來不會太乾。

I would like to get a pork chop. Medium well please.
我想來一份豬排，七分熟。

If I order the corn soup by itself, does it come with a drink?
單點玉米濃湯有附飲料嗎？

VOCABULARY：NUMBERS
常見的數字

1 ❶ **2** ❷ **3** ❸ **4** ❹

5 ❺ **6** ❻ **7** ❼ **8** ❽

1. 1 1 5. 5 5

2. 2 2 6. 6 6

3. 3 3 7. 7 7

4. 4 4 8. 8 8

DIY!
延虛線剪下訓練臂力與耐心

懶ㄉ分ㄌ

想下班

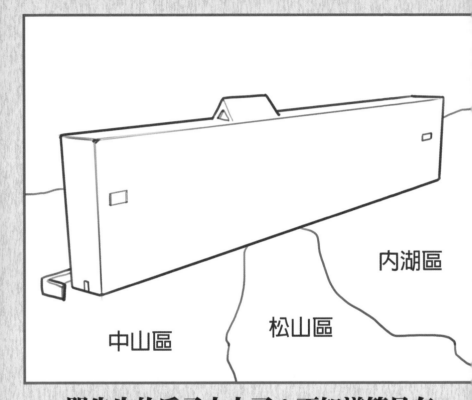

內湖區

松山區

中山區

關先生的房子太大了！不知道算是在
內湖區、中山區還是松山區。

**Mr. Guan's house is so big that it's
indistinguishable whether it's in
Zhongshan district, Neihu district or
Songshan district.**

district

區，轄區，地帶

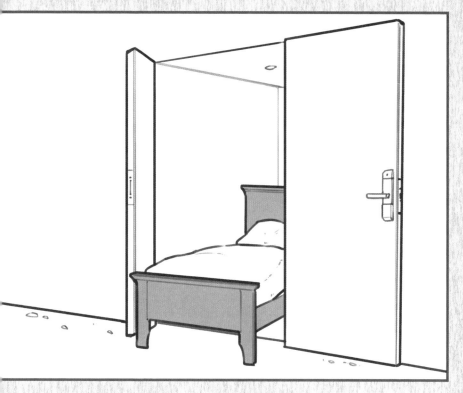

關先生的房子的牆蓋得太厚了！
連一張單人床都放不下。
The walls of Mr. Guan's house were built
so thick that it can't even fit a
twin sized bed!

thick

厚的；粗的

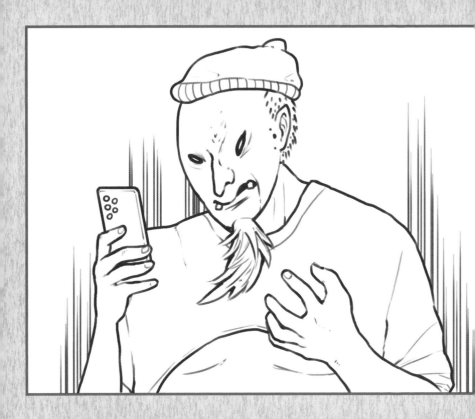

「我明明按了彈出式廣告的叉叉還是
跳到了廣告頁面！！！！」
"I Pressed the X on that pop-up ad and
it still OPENS THE AD!!!!! "

pop-up ad

彈出式廣告

「跑了七個ATM都寫已無存款！真倒楣。」
*"I've been to 7 ATMs and they all say
no balance left! Such bad luck."*

ATM

自動存提款機

如果你現在暴怒想要亂丟一個東西，
衛生紙並不是一個好選擇。

If you are pissed and have to throw
something, tissue is not a good choice.

tissue

衛生紙

天氣太冷了！
火山爆發只噴出冰塊！
It's too cold! The volcano erupted and only ice cubes came out!

erupt
噴出；爆發

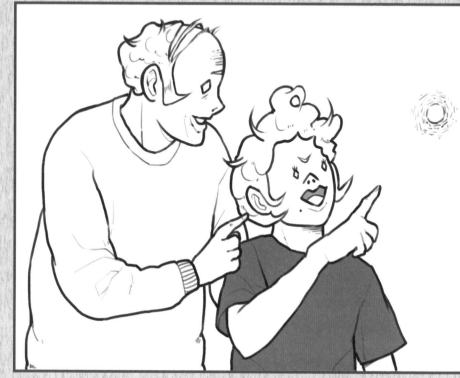

「爸，為什麼不管去哪太陽都一直跟著我們哇？
「等你長大後，稅、帳單、
房租、學貸也會一直跟著你唷。」

"Dad, why does the sun follow us everywhere?"
"When you grow up, taxes, bills, rent and
student loans will follow you everywhere too."

sun

太陽

Tammy是世界上最樂觀的人！
她相信有一天可以看到獵人的完結篇。

**Tammy is the most optimistic
person in the world!
She believes that she will one day
see the ending of Hunter x Hunter.**

optimistic

樂觀的

「我在尋找背寬38.7公分的男人，
他是在我出生時分開的孿生兄長…
啊！哥哥…？！」

"I'm looking for a man whose back width
is 38.7 cm. He is my twin brother who was
separated at birth...AH!!! Brother...?!"

back width

背寬

在海邊游泳時不小心睡著了，
醒來的時候已經游到了復活島。
I accidentally fell asleep while
swimming at the beach.
When I woke up,
I had reached Easter Island.

Easter Island

復活島

145

VOCABULARY：SANDWICH
三明治的常見單字

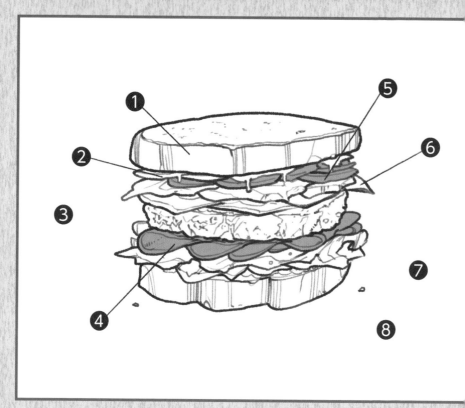

1. proton 質子
2. neutron 中子
3. air 空氣
4. Ant-Man 蟻人

5. electron 電子
6. cell wall 細胞壁
7. particulate matter 懸浮微粒
8. photon 光子

實用句子：飛機之旅

I want to get off at the next stop.
我下一站要下車。

Help! I cannot fit my kid in my baggage.
幫幫忙！我的小孩塞不進行李裡。

The captain and the first officer are taking pitcures with me! What an honor.
機長跟副機長同時來跟我合照！好榮幸。

Oh no, I forgot to bring my bomb with me!
噢不，我忘了帶我的炸彈了！

DIY!
延虛線剪下訓練臂力與耐心

實用篇

多益必考！指考學測一次搞定！

實用篇

BONUS：找不同

你好啊，真沒想到你可以看到這裡呢，
不過就到此為止了，
接下來是考驗眼球的時間！

SPOT THE DIFFERENCE! #1
請找出這兩張圖片中7個不一樣的地方。

SPOT THE DIFFERENCE! #1

請找出這兩張圖片中7個不一樣的地方。

SPOT THE DIFFERENCE! #2
請找出這兩張圖片中3個不一樣的地方

SPOT THE DIFFERENCE! #2
請找出這兩張圖片中3個不一樣的地方。

SPOT THE DIFFERENCE! #3
請找出這兩張圖片中20個不一樣的地方

SPOT THE DIFFERENCE! #3
找出這兩張圖片中20個不一樣的地方。

SPOT THE DIFFERENCE! #4
請找出這兩張圖片中1個不一樣的地方。

SPOT THE DIFFERENCE! #4
請找出這兩張圖片中1個不一樣的地方。

解答

SPOT THE DIFFERENCE! #1
請找出這兩張圖片中7個不一樣的地方。

SPOT THE DIFFERENCE! #2
請找出這兩張圖片中3個不一樣的地方

162

SPOT THE DIFFERENCE! #3

找出這兩張圖片中20個不一樣的地方。

SPOT THE DIFFERENCE! #4
請找出這兩張圖片中1個不一樣的地方。

後記

感謝各位看完這本
《鹽酥英語：讓你的的英語能力四分五裂》。
相信你的英語能力已經四分五裂了吧？

能製作出這本書，真的要感謝我的編輯國治。基本上他給了我 99.9999% 的自由來隨意發揮（你看到那個序有多隨便了嗎），而且還讓我瘋狂拖稿。
還記得第一次跟他開會時，我問：「所以，簽了這個約之後，在 12 月前我就一定要把整本書的內容都交給你對嗎？」他說：「是。」我接著問：「那如果我到 11 月 30 日時突然跟你說：『我不想出書嚕！掰。』會怎麼樣呢？」他說：「你不會怎樣，但我應該會死得很慘。」原來，這就是擁有別人生死權的感覺，於是我簽下了作者約。

除了編輯以外，也要特別感謝我哥蘑菇凍。
他總是能點石成金，這本書的每一頁都要經過他的審核我才敢收錄，有幾篇甚至是他原創的點子。
要是沒有他，這本書……應該也不會到多糟，但反正會比較無聊。
感謝我表姐髒腳蛇為了我頻道的影片配音尖叫多次，要是哪天她喉嚨受傷我可能要幫她出醫藥費。（但是美國看病好貴，噴。）還有幫我作曲的象牙汁跟鍋巴丸，其他配音過的親朋好友：香腿糕、尖高湯、酸蛙斬、皮包肉、鱉泥丼、鋼虎捲、蚌體鍋、軟糖蛋、星際瓜、皮蛋餃、燙沙拉、辣奶羹、辣肉桂、鶴喙堡、鹿餡絲。

也要大感謝 YouTuber 圈的朋友們，以及一直支持著我的每一個小餅乾，誠心的希望這本書不會因為銷受慘淡害編輯國治被上司開除，並且流落街頭。

Penguin Noodle

國家圖書館出版品預行編目（CIP）資料

Crispy Fried ABC鹽酥英語：讓你的英語能力四
分五裂/鵝肉麵作. -- 1版. -- 臺北市：城邦文化事
業股份有限公司尖端出版, 2021.01
　面；　公分
　ISBN 978-957-10-9348-2(平裝)
　1.英語　2.讀本
805.1892　　　　　　　　　　　　　109019765

Crispy Fried ABC鹽酥英語：讓你的英語能力四分五裂

作　　者／鵝肉麵
繪　　圖／鵝肉麵
創意協力／蘑菇凍

發 行 人／黃鎮隆
副總經理／陳君平
總 編 輯／洪琇菁
主　　編／楊國治
美術總監／沙雲珮
封面設計／陳又荻
協力美編／鍾睿紘、劉淳溽
活動企劃／邱小祐、劉宜蓉
廣告專線／（02）2500-7600／楊國治（分機1438）

出版
城邦文化事業股份有限公司　尖端出版
台北市104中山區民生東路二段141號10樓
電話／（02）2500-7600　傳真／（02）2500-1979
網址／www.spp.com.tw
E-mail／marketing@spp.com.tw
客服信箱E-mail／digi_camera@mail2.spp.com.tw

發行
英屬蓋曼群島商家庭傳媒股份有限公司城邦分公司　尖端出版
台北市104中山區民生東路二段141號10樓
電話／（02）2500-7600　傳真／（02）2500-1979

法律顧問
元禾法律事務所　地址／台北市羅斯福路三段37號15樓

書籍訂購
網址／www.spp.com.tw
劃撥專線／（03）312-4212
戶名／英屬蓋曼群島商家庭傳媒股份有限公司城邦分公司
帳號／50003021

國內經銷商
中彰投以北（含宜花東）經銷商／槍彥有限公司
電話／（02）8919-3369
傳真／（02）8914-5524
地址／231新北市新店區寶興路45巷6弄7號5樓
物流中心／231新北市新店區寶興路45巷6弄12號1樓
嘉義（雲嘉以南）經銷商／威信圖書有限公司
地址／600嘉義市文化路855號
電話／（05）233-3852
客服專線／0800-028-028
高雄經銷商／威信圖書有限公司
地址／814高雄縣仁武鄉考潭村成功路127-6號
客服專線／0800-028-028

海外經銷商
馬新／城邦（馬新）出版集團　Cite（M）Sdn Bhd
電話／603-9057-8822
傳真／603-9057-6622
E-mail／cite@cite.com.my
香港／城邦（香港）出版集團　Cite（H.K）Publishing Group Limi
電話／2508-6231
傳真／2578-9337
E-mail／hkcite@biznetvigator.com

版次／2021年1月1版1刷